This book belongs to:

_____

To

Mom and Dad,

Dawn,

Avery, Gabe, Emma, Sarah,

Darren.

I thank God for your inspiring presence in my life

And for every good thing

Including this book.

THE TRICKY, STICKY ADDICTION MONSTER

by

Charlaine Sevigny

This is Sam's mom. Sam used to live with his mom, and she loved him and took care of him. They did everything together.

But sometimes Sam's mom was sad. Sam didn't know why.

One day, when she was looking for a way to be happy, Sam's mom met the tricky, sticky Addiction Monster.

The Addiction Monster is a monster that lies and cheats and tricks people .

The tricky, sticky addiction Monster put on its best costume. It pretended to be fun and happy so Sam's mom would get close. The Addiction Monster smiled and danced and told her that it would make everything better.
   But it lied.

The Addiction Monster tells people that things like pills or alcohol, shopping, or gambling will help them be happy. But that's not true.

When Sam's mom followed the Addiction Monster, she got too close. It wrapped its slimy tentacles around her and covered her eyes.

Mom couldn't see anymore.

She couldn't see how much Sam missed her, or that he needed her. All she could see was the darkness of the tricky, sticky Addiction Monster.

That made Sam sad. He missed his mom. Sometimes he thought his mom didn't care about him anymore, but that was a lie. The Addiction Monster was getting in the way.

The monster wrapped one sticky tentacle around Mom's mouth and stole her smile. It took her voice too. Sometimes Mom was quiet and didn't talk to Sam. Sometimes the Monster threw a loud and angry version of mom's voice at Sam.

Sam felt scared when his mom got quiet and he felt scared when his mom yelled. Sam didn't know what to expect.

Sam's mom was confused by the Addiction Monster.

The Addiction Monster used one tentacle to steal mom's money. She didn't even notice it was gone. She couldn't pay the bills or buy groceries.

The monster used the long black tentacles to plug Mom's ears too. Suddenly she couldn't hear Sam crying, and she couldn't hear the people around her that wanted to help.

She couldn't hear the friends or doctors or counsellors. The Monster's tentacles stopped her from getting help.

Sometimes Sam's mom tried to get away from the Addiction Monster, but its tentacles were sticky and stretchy. Even when everyone thought she had escaped, the awful Monster pulled her right back... SNAP!

Mom was so tired from the struggle. Even though she loved Sam, she just couldn't take care of him.

Now Sam is staying with some people that want to keep him safe while his mom wrestles with the Addiction Monster. They are nice people.

They don't say bad things about his mom. They know the bad guy is the tricky, sticky Addiction Monster.

The Addiction Monster likes to hide, likes to be a dark secret. It lies to moms, dads, teenagers, grandparents, and friends. Sam isn't alone. Lot's of people are affected by the Addiction Monster and it's okay to talk about it.

Sometimes the Addiction Monster takes special people away forever. They might change so much because of those slimy tentacles that you don't even know who they are anymore.

But sometimes those special people can get away from the lies. It's very hard to do, but sometimes it happens.

Sam doesn't know if his mom will be able to get away from the Addiction Monster. He wishes he could save her, but he can't.

None of this is his fault.

Sam will keep on loving his Mom and do his best to grow up strong and healthy. He will find safe people to talk to about his feelings, and he will laugh and smile and play.

Sam will remember to always stay away from the Addiction Monster and its lies. That's the best gift he can give his mom.

To the grownups,

Addiction can be a hard thing to talk about. Thank you for taking the time to help kids understand what is happening in their lives. I've included some discussion questions with answers that you are welcome to use as a jumping point for conversation with the young ones in your company. If they don't know the answer take that chance to look back through the book together and find it. Be blessed, you most certainly are a blessing.

Addiction is when someone has the urge to do something that is hard to stop, even if it is harmful to them.

✏️ Q: Who can struggle with addiction?
A: Anyone, teens, adults, grandparents, friends...

✏️ Q: What lie did the Tricky Sticky Addiction Monster tell Sam's mom?
A: That it would make everything better.

✏️ Q: Did the monster make everything better?
A: No

Q: What were some of the things that happened to Sam's Mom, and how did Sam feel?

A: Mom couldn't see that Sam was sad, she couldn't hear people try to help. She lost all of her money. She lost her smile and sometimes yelled at Sam, or didn't talk to him at all. Sam was sad, he wondered if his mom had stopped caring about him.

Q: Have you ever felt like Sam? When?

A:

Q: Did Sam's mom love him?

A: Yes

Q: Did Sam make his mom sad or mad?

A: No

 Q: Could Sam save his mom from the Tricky Sticky Addiction Monster?

A: No

 Q: What is the best gift that Sam could give his mom?

A: To be happy and healthy and stay away from Addiction.

Made in the USA
Las Vegas, NV
15 January 2024

84439256R00021